Taffy Pulling

The book is based on my fond memories
of my childhood in the 1920s;
many of the settings, scenes and characters
in the book represent my house,
my pets and my children's dolls.
—*Tasha Tudor*

In memory of Owyn Corgi

Library of Cogress Cataloging-in-Publication Data

Tudor, Tasha
Corgiville Christmas / by Tasha Tudor-1st U.S. ed.
p. cm.
Summary: The inhabitants of Corgiville, including recent arrivals,
participate in a variety of activities in preparation for Christmas.
ISBN 1-932425-00-4 (alk. paper)
[1. Dogs-Fiction. 2. Animals-Fiction. 3. Christmas-Fiction.] I. Title.

PX7.T8228CK 2003
[E]-dc21   2003051412

Front Street
Asheville, North Carolina

CORGIVILLE CHRISTMAS

BY
TASHA TUDOR

W hen the snow geese fly south, and the far hills are white with snow, everyone in Corgiville turns their thoughts to Christmas.

Now is the time for delightful tea parties in front of the fire.

Mr. and Mrs. Brown enjoy their morning tea by the woodstove on chilly days.

A lot of time is spent making cornucopias for the tree,
painting Advent calendars, and marking off the days until Christmas.

The rabbits use kale,
as it is economical and
can be eaten later.

Of course the cats
prefer catnip wreaths,
mixed with cheese
balls, to attract mice.

On December sixth, the Bigbee Browns put up their Advent calendars
and light their Advent wreath, made from boxwood greens, which do not
shed needles into the teacups below, as spruce and balsam do.

Dundee cake is brought out from the pantry, where it has been aging since October. It is always served for tea on December sixth.

This year three new families have come to live in Corgiville.
The first family to arrive was Mr. Chickahominy, with his mother-in-law
Mrs. Eppycackle, and his two wives, Egglinetine Cluck and Nestacropsy.

They moved into a house overlooking the pond. The Browns and other neighbors helped them get settled. Chickahominy was enterprising, and opened an outstanding shop, Chickahominy's Haberdashery, which carries everything Corgiville families need.

Before Christmas, Chickahominy advertises his wares by driving his peddler's wagon all about Corgiville. It is the delight of daring corgi pups to hitch a ride. Great fun!

He is welcomed when he stops, as he has so many useful household items with which to tempt customers who can't get to the village when the snow lies too deeply on the back roads.

He does a tremendous business over the holiday season and offers a ten percent discount on all goods purchased during the Twelve Days of Christmas.

The second family to come to Corgiville is of Pennsylvania Dutch descent.

They hired Ishmael Crow to move them.

ISHMAEL CROW INC.
EXPERT MOVERS
AND
STORERS OF
HOUSEHOLD GOODS
CONTACT US AT THE NEST

The two Stauffer brothers, Abraham and Isaac, are both pharmacists, and their three sisters are skilled in herbal cures.

They, too, opened a shop—an excellent apothecary and
soda fountain next to Chickahominy's Haberdashery.

Isaac Stauffer's catnip milk shakes are very popular with the Purrer sisters, Puss and Minou. And Edgar Tomcat doesn't hesitate to order five at one sitting!

Isaac Stauffer makes superb ice cream, and already knows the favorite choices of all the corgi puppies, kittens, and young rabbits, for miles around.

Abraham Stauffer is amazingly helpful to ailing kittens and corgi pups. The rabbits are a bit hesitant to use his castor oil, and prefer the Stauffer sisters' herbal remedies.

The third family to come were the Cardigan Corgwyns of Wales.
They sport long tails, a novelty in Corgiville.
They are very socially minded, and gracious to their guests.

Their home is very tasteful, and to attend their parties gives one a certain "tone."
As they travel a lot, they have many interesting incidents to relate. They also collect
fine china and silver nutmeg graters and salt glaze crocks with owls on them.

Mert's Factory, The Boggs, is putting forth clouds of steam. He makes no end of enchanting toys at this season of the year. Everyone is eager to see his latest idea of fun at the Christmas Bazaar.

The church bazaar sells Mert's toys, especially his toy skunks and steam engines. There are lots of good things to eat as well. Snap's Bakery is very popular, as is Stauffer's Ice Cream.

When the pond freezes, so many skating parties, picnics,
and bonfires at night are a joyous part of Christmas.

It is now only a few days until December twenty-third, when the trip to The Christmas Woods is taken, to fetch Christmas trees. It is a day's journey, so plenty of food is prepared. Large sleighs are brought out, and goats are hitched up for the outing.

Here they are racing to see who will get there first. Mert has made
skis for his Tin Lizzie, and usually wins, though Chickahominy gives him
sharp competition skijoring with Caleb Brown's son, Farley.

They return by moonlight and lanterns after a wonderful day.

How welcoming is the sight of a warm home and the prospect of tea!
They have a perfect tree, and anticipate another happy Christmas.

At last, on the evening of December twenty-fifth, the door to the best parlor is opened. There stands the Christmas tree in its glory of lighted candles and shining ornaments. Everyone is silent with wonder, encircling the tree to wish all of you MERRY CHRISTMAS!